NEARLY NONSENSE

Hoja Tales from Turkey

Rina Singh

Illustrated by Farida Zaman

Tundra Books

Published in Canada by Tundra Books,
75 Sherbourne Street, Toronto, Ontario M5A 2P9

Published in the United States by Tundra Books of Northern New York,
P.O. Box 1030, Plattsburgh, New York 12901

Library of Congress Control Number: 2010928809

LIBRARY AND ARCHIVES CANADA CATALOGUING IN PUBLICATION

Singh, Rina, 1955-
Nearly nonsense : Hoja tales from Turkey / Rina Singh ;
illustrated by Farida Zaman.

ISBN 978-0-88776-974-0

1. Nasreddin Hoca (Legendary character) – Juvenile literature.
2. Tales – Turkey – Juvenile literature. I. Zaman, Farida II. Title.

PN6231.N27N42 2011   j398.2209561   C2010-903183-0

We acknowledge the financial support of the Government of Canada through the Book Publishing Industry Development Program (BPIDP) and that of the Government of Ontario through the Ontario Media Development Corporation's Ontario Book Initiative. We further acknowledge the support of the Canada Council for the Arts and the Ontario Arts Council for our publishing program.

ONTARIO ARTS COUNCIL
CONSEIL DES ARTS DE L'ONTARIO

Design: Jennifer Lum
Printed and bound in China

For Neela and Liloo, who make a lot of sense. — R.S.

To Rizwan, my travel companions. — F.Z.

CONTENTS

INTRODUCTION

Long ago in Turkey, there lived a man named Nasrudin Hoja. He was a mullah, a Muslim teacher, and he had as many lessons to learn as he had to teach.

No matter what the question, Hoja always had an answer. At times, he was caught doing the most foolish things, like trying to catch the moon. But he quickly twisted the situation in such a way that he looked wiser than ever – or at least he tried to.

He was a busy man. He worked at the vineyard, gave sermons at the mosque, and sometimes he was asked to be a judge in small courts. He was also a companion to the great Tamerlane from time to time. As if that wasn't enough, Hoja also had to deal with a nagging wife (who gave him long shopping lists), uninvited visitors (who were forever dropping in), and assorted animals (mostly donkeys).

His life was hard, his problems many, but he dealt with his daily mishaps with a light heart. Like the time he lost his donkey, and neighbors dropped by to say how sorry they were to hear the news.

He dismissed their sympathies and said, "It's a good thing the wretched beast got lost."

"What do you mean?" asked the confused neighbors.

"Imagine if I were riding the donkey at the time – I'd be lost too."

On the surface, these tales may seem like jokes, but there is a hidden wisdom to each that Sufis (Muslim mystics) use to illustrate their teachings.

Although the stories may have changed with time, Hoja has remained constant – the endearing fool, an impossible trickster, and a beloved character of Turkish folktales.

DONKEY TROUBLE

One morning, Hoja's wife handed him a list of things to buy from the marketplace – sugar, spices, vegetables, rice, coffee . . . . The list went on and on.

"What do we need so many things for?" Hoja muttered to himself. Knowing very well that there was no way out of this weekly chore, he asked his son to get the donkey ready. He mounted the donkey and his son walked ahead.

They were only a little way into their journey when they met two passersby.

"Look at Hoja!" exclaimed the men. "He rides like a king and his poor son walks like a servant. Tch, tch, tch."

Hoja blushed with shame, brought the donkey to a standstill, and climbed down.

"Son, why don't you ride the donkey for the rest of the way?" he suggested.

The boy obediently mounted the donkey and they resumed their trek to the marketplace.

As they walked on, they met some neighbors.

"What's happening to this world, Hoja?" they asked. "The poor father walks in the heat while the son rides the donkey like a prince. Tch, tch, tch."

The poor boy, overcome with guilt, climbed down from the donkey at once.

Hoja decided they should both walk with the donkey. *That should shut up the busybodies*, he thought.

The morning was getting hotter, and they were not even halfway when a bunch of youngsters saw them and began to laugh hysterically.

"Look! Look! The two fools of Akşehir are walking to the marketplace," said one boy.

"If I had a donkey," said another, "I would be riding it, not taking it for a stroll." The group broke into fresh peals of laughter.

Hoja pretended to ignore the hoodlums, but when they were out of earshot, he said to his son, "They do have a point. What's the use of owning a donkey if we can't ride it? We will both ride the donkey."

With some difficulty, they climbed onto the donkey and squeezed themselves into the saddle. And that's how they resumed their journey.

As they came closer to the marketplace, they were stopped by a group of elderly men.

"Hoja," said one of the men in a scolding voice, "have you no pity for animals? The donkey is also Allah's creature. How can it carry the weight of two people? Tch, tch, tch."

To be chided in front of his son by a bunch of illiterate men upset Hoja. The only thing left to do was to carry the troublesome donkey on their shoulders. And that's just what they did, much to the amusement of the shoppers and vendors. All this donkey business put Hoja in a very bad mood.

THE SLAP

As Hoja stood in the middle of the marketplace, reading his shopping list, a man approached him and – without as much as a greeting – slapped him in the face.

Hoja staggered but composed himself quickly. "What's the meaning of this?" he demanded angrily.

"I beg your pardon, sir," said the stranger apologetically. "I mistook you for a friend who looks just like you."

Hoja was in no mood to accept such nonsensical explanations. But the stranger insisted that he always greeted his friend like that. He had apologized, and, as far as the stranger was concerned, the matter was over.

But you and I know that the matter was far from over.

A crowd gathered around the two men. Those who didn't know Hoja asked him to let the man go, but those who knew him from the village fueled his fires.

"Take him to the judge. Let him pay the price for insulting a mullah – a crime made worse by doing so in public," they said, raising their voices. But Hoja's fires needed no fueling. He grabbed the offender by the wrist and marched him to the courthouse.

When it was their turn to meet with the judge, they each told their version of the story.

"You have been wronged, and you should get justice," the judge said to Hoja. And to the offender, the judge's verdict was simple, which he delivered with a wink and a slight nod. "I order you to pay four *ghurush* (Turkish coins used in the thirteenth century) to Hoja for slapping him."

Hoja noticed the odd way the verdict was delivered, for he himself had served as the town judge from time to time, but he thought nothing of it as long as justice was done.

The stranger patted his pockets dramatically and said he had no coins with him. The judge granted him permission to go home and bring back the four coins immediately.

Hoja waited and waited. Minutes turned into an hour and there was still no sign of the man. Hoja remembered the wink, and his suspicion that the judge and the stranger might be friends was confirmed. He knew now that he would not get any justice.

He went up to the judge and asked very respectfully, "Do I understand correctly that four *ghurush* is a fair payment for a slap in the face?"

"That's what I said," answered the judge.

Hoja took one step closer and slapped the judge in the face.

"What is the meaning of this?" shouted the judge, rubbing his cheek.

"I have some shopping to finish. Why don't you keep the four coins when your friend returns?" said Hoja, and he walked out of the courthouse with his head held high.

THE SERMON

Every Friday, Hoja was invited to the mosque to deliver a sermon. There were some Fridays when he had a lot to say, but then there were other Fridays when nothing came to his mind. That could be worrisome.

One such Friday, Hoja woke up and looked at his donkey, who was staring at him silently. He looked at his wife, who was fussing over household chores and complaining about her lot. He looked at his breakfast, which didn't say much at all. He walked to the front door and looked outside at people rushing back and forth on the street, trying to finish their errands before prayer time. Nothing seemed to be of any great importance that morning. His mind felt as empty as that of his own little donkey.

He put on his coat and his turban, and he walked to the

mosque. If he was worried, it didn't show.

He walked through the mosque door, mounted the platform, cleared his throat, and addressed the congregation.

"Friends," he began solemnly. "Do you know what today's sermon is about?" He folded his arms and waited.

The people shook their heads, and Hoja paused and gave everyone a perplexed look.

"Oh, learned people," he began again. "Surely you must have some idea of what I'm about to share with you?"

People's heads shook again, collectively this time.

"I can't believe it, that I'm actually invited to speak to a bunch of such ignorant people," exclaimed Hoja with exasperation. And then with the swish of his robe and a little tuck to the turban, he stepped down and walked out of the mosque, shaking his own head in mock disbelief.

The people were dumbfounded. They rolled up their mats quietly and went home.

There was no doubt in Hoja's mind that by the following Friday he would have some inspiration, some great thoughts, some valuable advice to share with the people. But Friday arrived and Hoja's brain felt as empty as his donkey's. News of the previous week's strange incident had spread, and – out of curiosity – more people went to the mosque to see what Hoja was up to.

Hoja arrived at the mosque, mounted the platform, and cleared his throat. And you are not going to believe it, but he started his sermon by asking the exact same question.

"Friends," he said. "Do you know what today's sermon is about?"

People's heads nodded quite vigorously. They had obviously learned a lesson.

He looked at the nodding heads and smiled almost with relief. "Aha! I knew I was in the company of such learned people. In that case, I will not waste your precious time." And then with the swish of his robe and a little tuck to the turban, he stepped down and walked out of the mosque.

The people didn't quite believe that Hoja had walked away again without delivering the sermon. They rolled up their mats and went home, but they could hardly wait till next Friday to see how Hoja would get himself out of the hole he had dug.

Friday came again, and when Hoja walked into the mosque, he

could sense all eyes on him. He mounted the platform and cleared his throat. You are not going to believe it, but he started his sermon by asking the exact same question. But, you see, you can trick the people once and you can even trick them twice, but really you can't trick the people all the time.

"No," said the people who remembered the lesson from the previous week.

"Yes," said the people who recalled the lesson from the week before that.

"Aha!" said Hoja, rubbing his hands together with glee. He smiled. "Some of you know it and some of you don't. That's perfect!"

Hoja addressed the nodding heads very humbly. "You are more learned than I am. Kindly deliver the sermon to the ones who don't know." And then with the swish of his robe and a little tuck to the turban, Hoja stepped down and walked out of the mosque. Again.

He was free to go about his life just as he wanted – but only till the next Friday.

PUMPKINS AND WALNUTS

Hoja was walking home from the vineyard with his donkey one summer day. He felt so hot that he decided to take a rest. He stopped by a huge walnut tree that was growing beside a pumpkin patch. He tied his donkey to the tree and took off his turban to cool his head.

He gazed around, admiring the ripe pumpkins growing on slender vines and the walnuts hanging from big branches. He looked at the pumpkins and the walnuts again. Something didn't add up.

Strange are the ways of nature, he thought.

He looked up at the sky and couldn't stop from saying aloud,

"I think there has been a mistake. Don't you think the enormous pumpkins belong on this mighty tree and the puny walnuts in the ground on spindly vines?"

Of course, no one responded because no one was up there.

The more he thought about it, the more convinced he became that an error had been made by nature. So much thinking hurt his brain, and he drifted off to sleep, only to be woken by a hard object hitting his head.

For a moment he looked angrily at the ripe walnut that had hit him, and then at the tree as if it was to blame. But his anger subsided as soon as his eyes fell on the massive pumpkins nearby, and he cringed.

"Forgive me!" said Hoja, looking up at the sky gratefully. "What was I thinking? Of course the pumpkins are fine where they are in the ground and the walnuts most suitable to grow on the tree." The very thought of a pumpkin falling on his head from a tree cleared all doubts from his mind.

He untied the donkey and walked home, promising to mind his own business in the future.

HOJA AT THE BATHHOUSE

One day, Hoja went to the *hammam* (public bathhouse), a place where people of every rank, young or old, rich or poor, could visit. Hoja arrived in his shabby work clothes. The attendant ushered him in, took one look at his attire, and decided not to waste any more time on him.

The attendant handed him a worn out *pestemal* (a cloth to cover the body), an old towel, and *patens* (wooden clogs). Then he disappeared, probably to dote on better clients.

Hoja put on the *patens* and made his way to the steam room. No one came to scrub him or suggest a massage. No one offered him a drink of water or recommended that he cool down his body temperature before he went outside.

On his way out, Hoja sought out the attendant, thanked him, and tipped him with a gold coin. The attendant was pleasantly taken aback. Such a generous tip for the shameful service! He wished there were more stupid people like Hoja who would come to the *hammam*.

A week later, Hoja returned in the same scruffy clothes. The attendant, upon seeing Hoja, jumped to salute him. He fetched a spanking new *pestemal* and a fresh, crisp towel. He escorted him to the steam room.

With a *kese* (scrubbing glove), the attendant scoured the dust out of Hoja's pores. He then gave him a massage with scented oil. He even helped him with his bath by pouring water on him. He served him a drink while he cooled down.

On his way out, Hoja took out some (very) small change and gave it to the attendant.

The attendant was taken aback, but this time he was disappointed.

"Hoja," he said, pointing to the meager tip in his palm. "Was anything wrong with the service today?"

"Oh, no," said Hoja. "The service was excellent, but I already tipped you for to-day's service. This tip is for last week's service."

RABBIT SOUP

A man from a neighboring village came to Akşehir for business. He was a mere acquaintance of Hoja, so you can imagine Hoja's surprise when the man showed up at his door.

"For you, Hoja," he said, handing him a rabbit. Hoja was pleased with the gift.

And, as is the Turkish custom, Hoja invited the man in. He asked his wife to prepare a meal for their guest.

For dinner, Hoja served rabbit stew.

A few days later, some more people came to Akşehir for business. They too showed up at Hoja's door. They were total strangers, and they came empty-handed.

They quickly introduced themselves. "We are relatives of the man who brought you the rabbit a few days ago."

"Ah, the rabbit," exclaimed Hoja. And, as is the Turkish custom, he invited them in. All four of them. He asked his wife to prepare a meal.

For dinner, Hoja served rabbit soup.

"This is the broth of the rabbit your relative brought," said Hoja, pointing to the watery soup that left the guests disappointed and hungry.

But that didn't stop another batch of total strangers from showing up at Hoja's door a few days later. (They didn't bring any gifts either). They hastily introduced themselves.

"We are friends of the relatives of the man who brought you the rabbit," they said.

"Ah, the rabbit," said Hoja.

And since no one is turned away from a Turkish home, Hoja invited them in. He gave instructions to his wife to prepare a meal.

For dinner, Hoja served hot water in soup bowls.

"What is this?" asked the guests, offended by the insult.

"This is the broth of the broth of the rabbit that your friends' relatives' relative brought," said Hoja, putting an end to the stream of unwelcome guests.

THE FOUR ARROWS

One day, Tamerlane sent for Hoja to accompany him to the grounds where his soldiers were practicing archery. Hoja's company always made the day go faster.

Hoja gladly accepted the royal invitation – anything was better than planting tomatoes in his own garden.

It was a beautiful day, and Hoja felt good about himself.

"Reminds me of my days as an archer," boasted Hoja to Tamerlane as they watched the soldiers.

"You, an archer?" exclaimed Tamerlane.

Hoja then began to speak from both sides of his mouth. "Never missed a target," he bragged.

Tamerlane got all excited and commanded his soldiers to bring a bow and an arrow so Hoja could show the incompetent fools a trick or two.

"Oh, no, no, no!" protested Hoja. "I wouldn't dream of wasting their practice time." Hoja came up with every excuse he could think of in a hurry. "Not today." "I twisted my finger this morning." "It's been such a long time."

But a command is a command, and Hoja was expected to obey – or else. So Hoja picked up the bow and arrow. From the side of his eyes, he darted a quick glance at the soldiers to see how they were holding the bow and arrow. He first squinted, and then he closed both his eyes and let the arrow go, hoping it would hit the target.

The arrow left the bow, but barely; it fell limply to the ground just two feet away.

Tamerlane was dying to see Hoja embarrassed. (He found that funny.)

But, with a smile, Hoja said, "That is how your soldiers shoot."

Hoja took another arrow and gave a mighty pull. The soldiers ducked for cover for they didn't know where the arrow would fall. Fortunately it hit no one, but unfortunately it met a similar fate as the first arrow.

"And that is how your chief of army shoots," said Hoja.

Hoja took the third arrow, and soldiers prepared to dodge again in any direction.

The third arrow did hit the target, but it was way off the mark.

"And that?" asked Tamerlane, who could hardly wait to burst Hoja's bubble.

"That is how your general shoots," said Hoja.

Emboldened by a little practice, Hoja confidently took another arrow and didn't even bother to squint. The arrow left the bow like a strike of lightning and lodged itself in the center of bull's-eye. For a brief moment, Hoja's jaw dropped, but he collected himself right away.

"And that is how Hoja shoots," said Hoja, shrugging his shoulders.

THE COAT

Hoja, like many of his friends and acquaintances in Akşehir, was invited to a banquet. His wealthy friend was famous for putting out sumptuous feasts.

Before leaving for the vineyard on the morning of the banquet, Hoja laid out his red silk coat, the one he wore when he was a courtier for Tamerlane and the one he saved for very special occasions. He also took out a sparkling new turban for the evening.

Hoja had a rough day at the vineyard and ended up staying a little longer than usual. When he was returning home, he saw many people already dressed and leaving for the party. Hoja estimated that by the time he went home, took a bath, dressed himself, and headed out again, he would be extremely late for the feast. He

looked down at his coat. It had patches upon patches. He dusted it so it didn't look so bad. He sniffed himself, and he smelled of soil, squashed grapes, and donkeys. But what's a little smell between friends? He decided to go to the banquet as he was, for he didn't want to miss any of the fun.

He tied his donkey to a tree outside his friend's house and went in. The doormen stared at him speechlessly as he walked past them. Once inside, he offered salutations to everyone he met. And for a few moments, nothing seemed amiss. Then he noticed that even his friends drew away when he tried to speak to them. The host ignored him completely and gushed over other guests. The servants didn't even bother to pass the trays with pistachio nuts and baklava in front of him or offer him a drink.

Hoja was not about to give up so easily. He slipped out, untied his donkey, and rushed home.

"Hot water, please!" he ordered his wife.

He poured salt crystals into his hot bath and he scrubbed away the day's dirt from his skin till he was shining clean.

He put on his red silk coat, changed his turban, and wore embroidered shoes with curled toes. Then he trekked back to the banquet.

The doormen ushered him in. The people nodded and acknowledged him as he made a grand appearance. The servants escorted him to the host's table, and he sat down. Hoja, who was never shy, jumped right into the conversation, adding his own flair and wisdom. He stopped mid-sentence, unbuttoned his coat, and reached out for a juicy lamb chop. Instead of eating it, he stuffed it into the inner pocket of the coat.

"Eat, coat, eat!" he ordered, and then he continued with the story he had been telling.

The baffled guests stopped eating and stared at him in astonishment.

Now that Hoja had the full attention of the guests, he spoke even more eloquently. He stopped every now and then to reach for food. He scooped up rice pilaf and put it in the outer pocket. "Eat, coat, eat!" he repeated.

He slipped a pickle into the folds of his turban and packed some sticky baklava in another pocket.

The host was aghast at such terrible table manners. "What do you mean by this, Hoja?" he scolded him. "Why are you wasting my fine food to feed your coat?"

"Surely you don't mind," said Hoja. "When I came in my old coat, you offered me no hospitality at all, and now I wear this fine coat and you seat me at your table and nothing is good enough for me. It must be the coat you invited to the feast."

THE SMELL OF SOUP

Once, Hoja was a judge, and he was known to look at cases in ways no one else did, but somehow justice was done.

One day, a hungry beggar wandered the streets of Akşehir. It had been two days since food had passed his lips. He felt lucky when a generous vendor gave him a piece of day-old bread. As he was looking for a place to sit down to eat, he noticed a small restaurant. He walked over, hoping a kind owner might give him a bowl of soup to dip his bread in.

"Get away from here!" the restaurant owner shouted before the beggar could even utter his request.

"A little soup was all I was going to ask for," said the beggar.

"Get away before I call my men from the kitchen to give you a thrashing!" threatened the restaurant owner, afraid that the likes of the beggar would drive his other customers away. The beggar timidly walked away, turned the corner, and found the alley that led to the back of the restaurant where the open kitchen was.

Lamb stew simmered in one big pot on the stove, and lentil soup bubbled in another. The steam from the soup filled the air. The beggar quietly snuck near the pots, smelling the divine aromas, and waved his bread over the steam, hoping to soften it.

The owner saw him from inside the restaurant and came charging at him. "You thief! You're stealing my soup."

"I didn't even touch your soup; I was only smelling it," said the beggar, professing his innocence.

"Then you must pay for the smell of the soup," demanded the owner.

"If I had the money, I would buy your soup and not smell it," said the beggar, hoping it would be the end of the matter.

But the owner was enraged and seized the beggar by the collar and

dragged him to see Hoja, who was serving as a town judge at the time.

Hoja listened to the owner's complaint and to the beggar's defense, and he pondered deeply.

"So you demand payment for the smell of soup?" he asked to confirm.

"Absolutely!" said the owner.

"How much does your soup cost?" asked Hoja.

"Three *ghurush*."

Hoja asked the beggar if he had the three coins. The beggar was dismayed at the prospect of losing his entire week's earnings, but he handed Hoja the coins.

Hoja signaled to the restaurant owner to come up close. When the owner did, Hoja jingled the coins. "What do you hear?" asked Hoja.

"The sound of money," said the owner.

"Do you hear it clearly?" asked Hoja.

He did.

"Aha!" said Hoja. "You can go home now. The smell of soup has been paid by the sound of money."

Hoja returned the money to the beggar and sent them both on their way.

THE THREE QUESTIONS

One time, the mayor of Akşehir received news that three wise men from another land would be passing through his town. In fact, a very pompous message preceded their visit:

> "We have traveled through many towns and met
> scholars and learned men, but unfortunately they
> could not answer our questions. It would be a
> pleasure to meet the wise men of your town."

The mayor panicked because he had a reputation to keep. He sent for Hoja. Hoja was delighted with the invitation. What a great way to spend an evening – in the company of wise men and later dining with them at the mayor's expense.

Hoja saddled his donkey and left for the mayor's house right away. When he got there, he saw that the wise men had already arrived and the show of wisdom was about to begin.

The wise men were dressed elaborately in velvet robes and big turbans, and they had long, flowing beards. They looked very distinguished indeed.

The three men sized him up, and Hoja wished he had changed his robe or at least washed his face.

"So this is Hoja, who you were telling us about?" they asked the mayor.

Hoja acknowledged their rude greeting.

"Why don't I start?" said the first wise man. "Hoja, where is the center of the earth?"

Hoja contemplated deeply, and he began to walk up and down, tapping his foot, giving the appearance of doing some serious calculations. He walked over to his donkey and did some more tapping.

"Right here," said Hoja, pointing to the spot where his donkey's front hoof was.

"How can you be so sure?" demanded the first wise man.

"You have every right to doubt, but that shouldn't stop you from cross-checking. Measure from this spot, and if you find it is a yard too less or a yard too many, you will be declared wiser than Hoja," he replied.

The wise man began to feel a little stupid and quickly motioned for the second wise man to ask his question.

The second wise man stepped forward with a conceited air, waiting to nail Hoja.

"How many stars are there in the sky?" he asked.

Hoja looked up and he looked at his donkey. He looked up again and looked at his donkey again, giving the appearance of doing some serious calculations.

"There are as many stars in the sky as there are hairs on my donkey," announced Hoja, with great finality.

What kind of dumb men did the town have? thought the second wise man. "And how do you know that?" he asked a bit abruptly.

"I did my calculations, but of course you don't have to take my word for it. Please go ahead and count the stars and the hairs on my donkey. If there is one too less or one too many, then all of Akşehir will know that you are wiser than Hoja," said Hoja.

The second wise man and the donkey stared at each other stupidly.

The second wise man stepped back and motioned for the third wise man to come forward.

The third wise man was the most overbearing of all, not only in his attire but with a matching wait-till-I-get-you expression as well.

"I have a very simple question for you," said the third wise man, hoping to stump the smart aleck. "How many hairs are there in my beard?" he asked, stroking his long, long, gray beard.

Hoja stepped a bit closer, squinted at his beard, and then examined his donkey's tail. He squinted at the beard again and then examined his donkey's tail again. And he kept this up for a while, giving the appearance of doing some serious calculations.

"There are as many hairs in your respected beard as there are hairs in my wretched donkey's tail," said Hoja.

This was too much of an insult. "What . . . what do you mean by that?" stammered the third wise man.

"But of course you don't have to take my word for it. Why don't you pull the hair out of my donkey's tail and I will pluck the hair from your chin and the most honorable mayor can count. If there is one hair too less or one too many, you can go from town to town, even land to land, and declare yourself wiser than Hoja," said Hoja.

The wise man lowered his eyes and retreated back to his companions, and Hoja wondered when the feast would begin.